Where is Skipper?

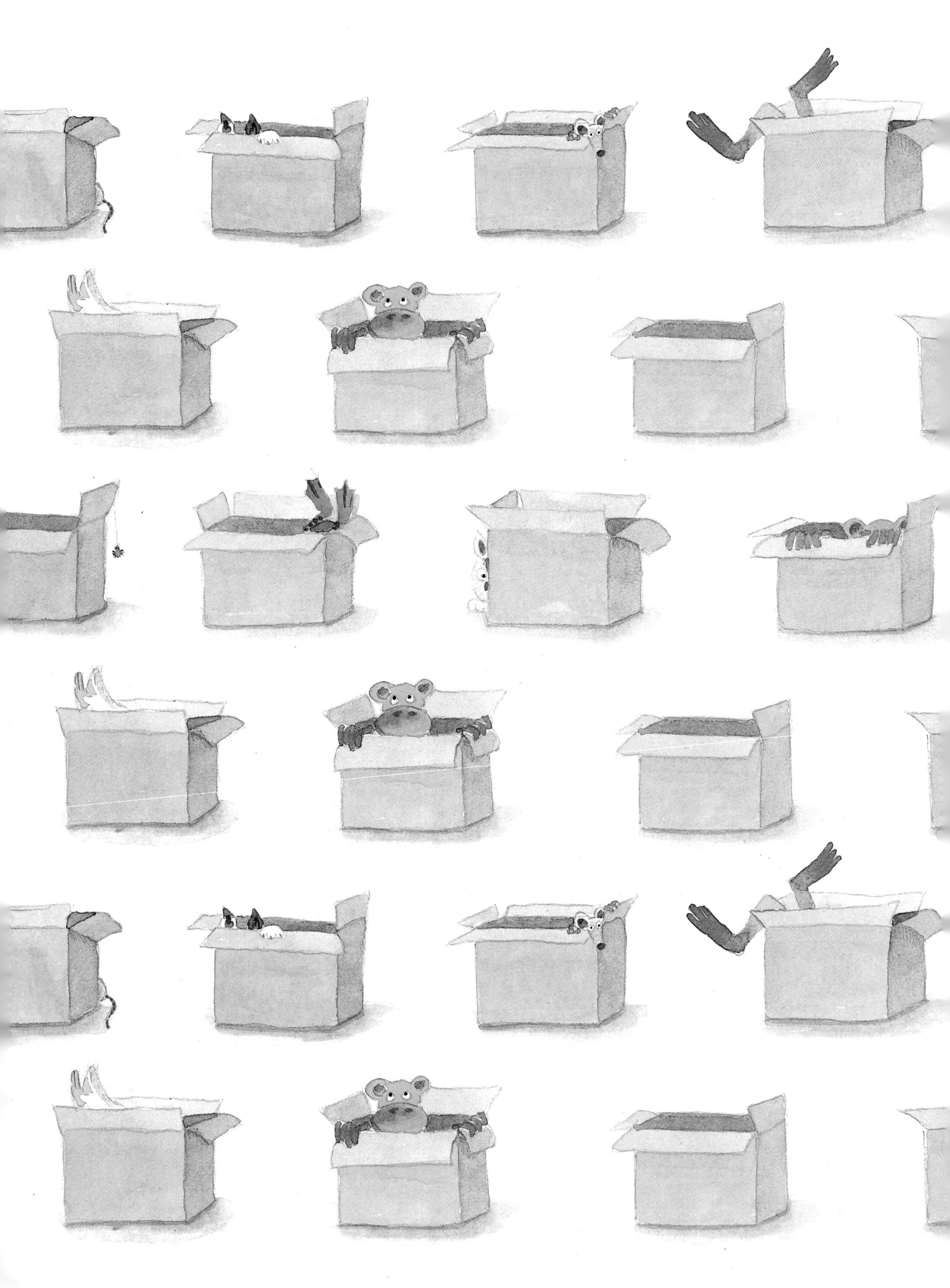

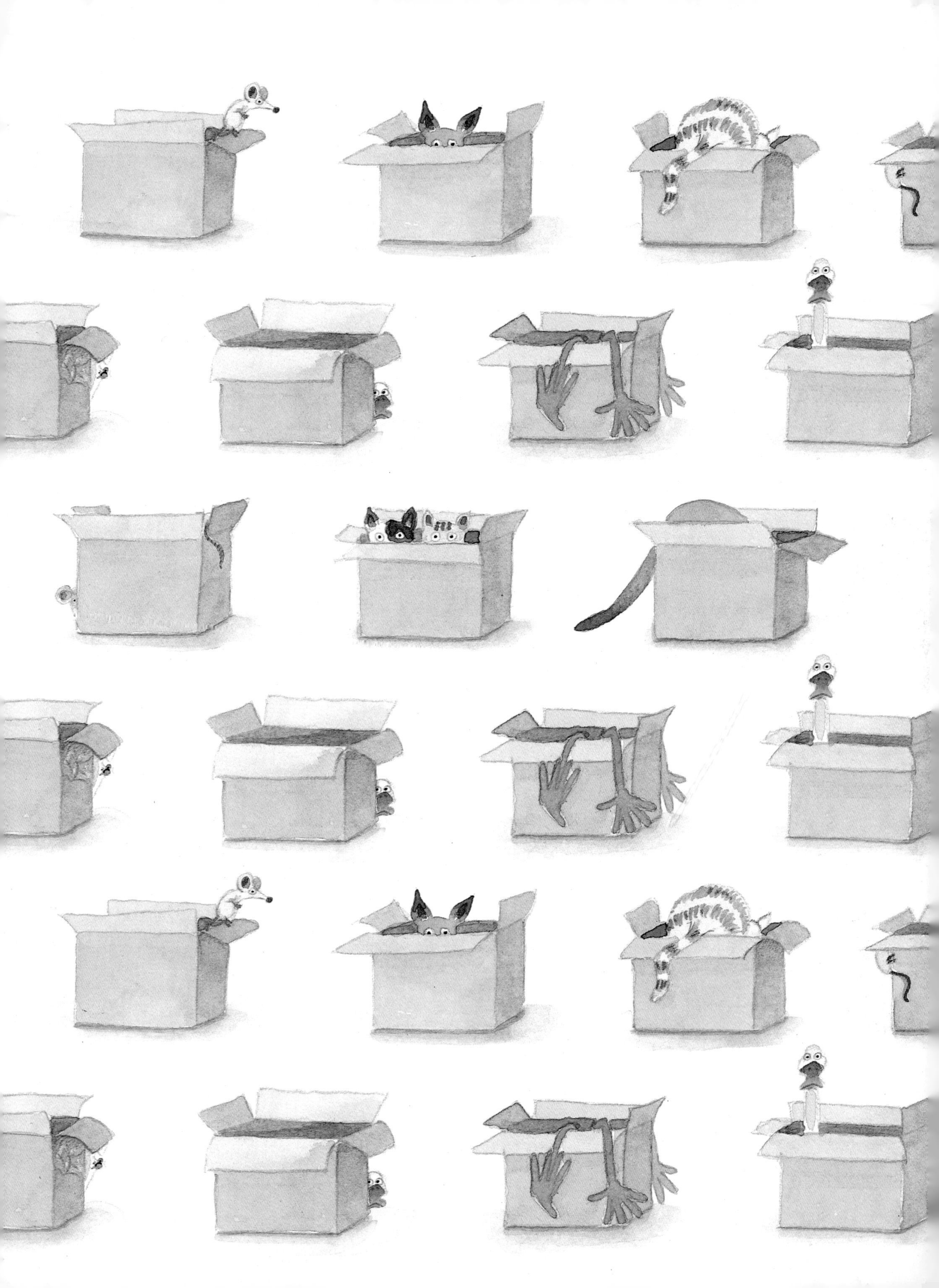

For Harry, whom I found

Nicolle

Where is Skipper?

Nicolle van den Hurk
(illustration)

Ivo de Wijs
(text)

Tjaart Theron
(translation)

Originally published in the Netherlands by Elzenga, Tilburg. The title of the Dutch edition is *Waar is Springer, waar is Twikkie?*
Translated from the Dutch by Tjaart Theron

All inquiries should be adressed to:
Barron's Educational Series, Inc.
250 Wireless Boulevard
Hauppauge, NY 11788

International Standard Book No. 0-8120-6360-0 (hardcover)
0-8120-1728-5 (paperback)

Library of Congress Catalog Card No. 93-10715

Library of Congress Cataloging-in-Publication Data

van den Hurk, Nicolle.
[Waar is Springer, waar is Twikkie? English]
Where is Skipper? / Nicolle van den Hurk, illustration, Ivo de Wijs, text ; Tjaart Theron, translation.
p. cm.
Summary: Jack and Michelle search all over the house for Skipper the kangaroo and Twinkle the cat and the reader is invited to help them look.
ISBN 0-8120-1728-5 (pbk.) — ISBN 0-8120-6360-0 (hard)
[1. Lost and found possessions—Fiction.] I. de Wijs, Ivo, text. II. Title.
PZ7.W6398Wh 1993
[E]—dc20 93-10715
CIP
AC

PRINTED IN HONG KONG
34567 4900 987654321

This is a search book.
It is about Jack and Michelle.
And about Skipper and Twinkle.

Look, here you see Jack with Michelle and Skipper.
But which is which?
You can try finding out!

Do you see Jack?
Is this the real Jack?
Do you see the real Michelle?
And do you see Skipper?
And do you see Twinkle, Michelle's cat?

"Play," Michelle whispers, "I want to play.
I want to play with Skipper and Twinkle.
But where are they?
Shall we go to look for them?
Where is Skipper, where is Twinkle?"

Jack shouts:
"Skipper! SKIPPER! S K I P P Y !"
And Michelle howls even louder:
"Twinkle! TWINKLE! T W I N K L E !"

No reply!
Skipper and Twinkle are *not*
in the kitchen.

“Come with me, we have to find them!
We’ll go to my room,
perhaps they are *there*.”

No.
Nothing.
Zilch.
Trouble.
No cat and *no* kangaroo.

"There's an ape," says Jack.
"That is Little Ape Snout," says Michelle.
"I'll ask if he wants to help look."

"Do you see your mother, Michelle?"
"No," sighs Michelle, "I only see Ducky Dee.
But as for the rest, I see nobody. Nobody at all."

“Where are the kangaroo and the cat?”
Michelle thinks.
“Where are the kangaraps,
the catgaroo, the kangapuss?
And where are Little Ape Snout and Ducky Dee?”

And Jack calls: "Skipper! Twinky!
Little Skipperoo!! Twinkypussy!!
Where could you be?"

"The hatch is shut," says Jack.
"They cannot be in the attic!
There are only mice in
the attic, Michelle!"

"I still want to have a
quick look!"
"Are they there?" asks Jack.
"I don't see them,"
says Michelle.
"I told you so!" says Jack.

“Where does Skipper come from?” asks Michelle.
“From a country far away,” says Jack.
“From Australia.”
“And Twinkle?”
“Twinkle comes from the A.S.P.C.A.,” says Michelle.

"Oh my, oh no," Michelle thinks.
"Maybe all animals have gone traveling.
To Australia or Espicalia.
Oh my, oh no, oh gee."

"Hey! Look!
Do you see the eyes glowing?
That must be Twinkle."

But no...it isn't Twinkle.
It is Patchy Tom, the neighbor's cat.
And Twinkle and Skipper are still gone.

Michelle puffs: “Pffff.”
And Jack puffs along with Michelle: “Pffffff.”
“We’ve been everywhere,” says Michelle.
“In the kitchen and the bedrooms.
In the attic and in the cellar...”
“Wait!
Stop!
We’ve forgotten one room!
Come with me!”

"Yes, yippee, *there* is
Skipper."
"Hello kangaroodear,"
Jack calls.
"But...where is Twinkle?"

"*There* is Twinkle!"
"Hello Twinkle, hello pouchpussy,"
Michelle says.
"Hello Little Ape Snout, hello Ducky Dee,
hello Patchy Tom, hello little spider,
hello mice.
Now we can go and play!"

"Yes, now we're going to play," says Jack. "But what?"
Skipper says nothing. Twinkle, too, says nothing.
And Ducky Dee keeps his beak shut.
And Michelle? Michelle thinks.
"Well, Michelle, what are we going to do?" Jack asks again.
Then Michelle says, very, very softly: "Jack, Jack, Jack,
Jack, little dearest...
I thought...maybe...
hide-and-seek!"

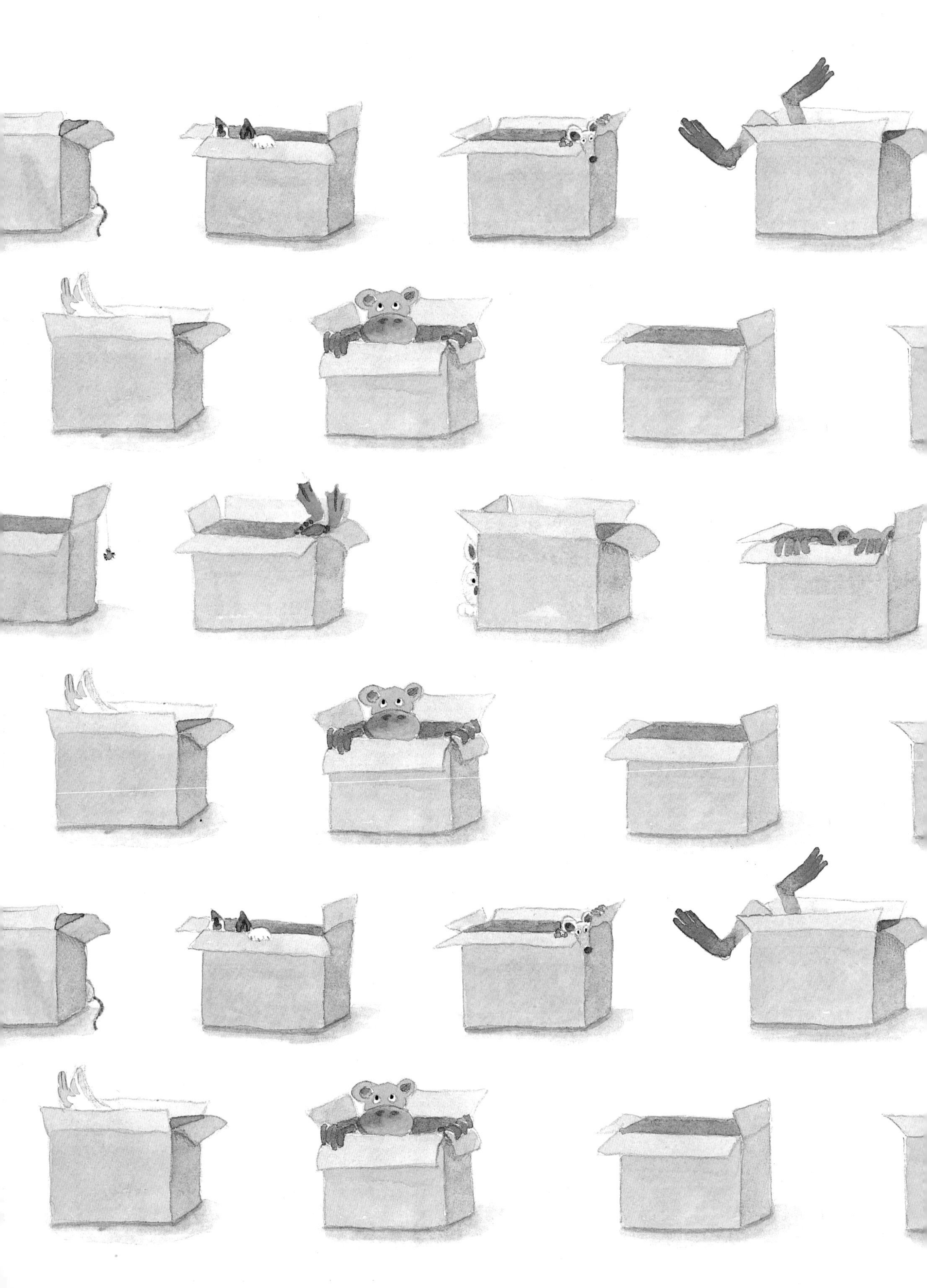

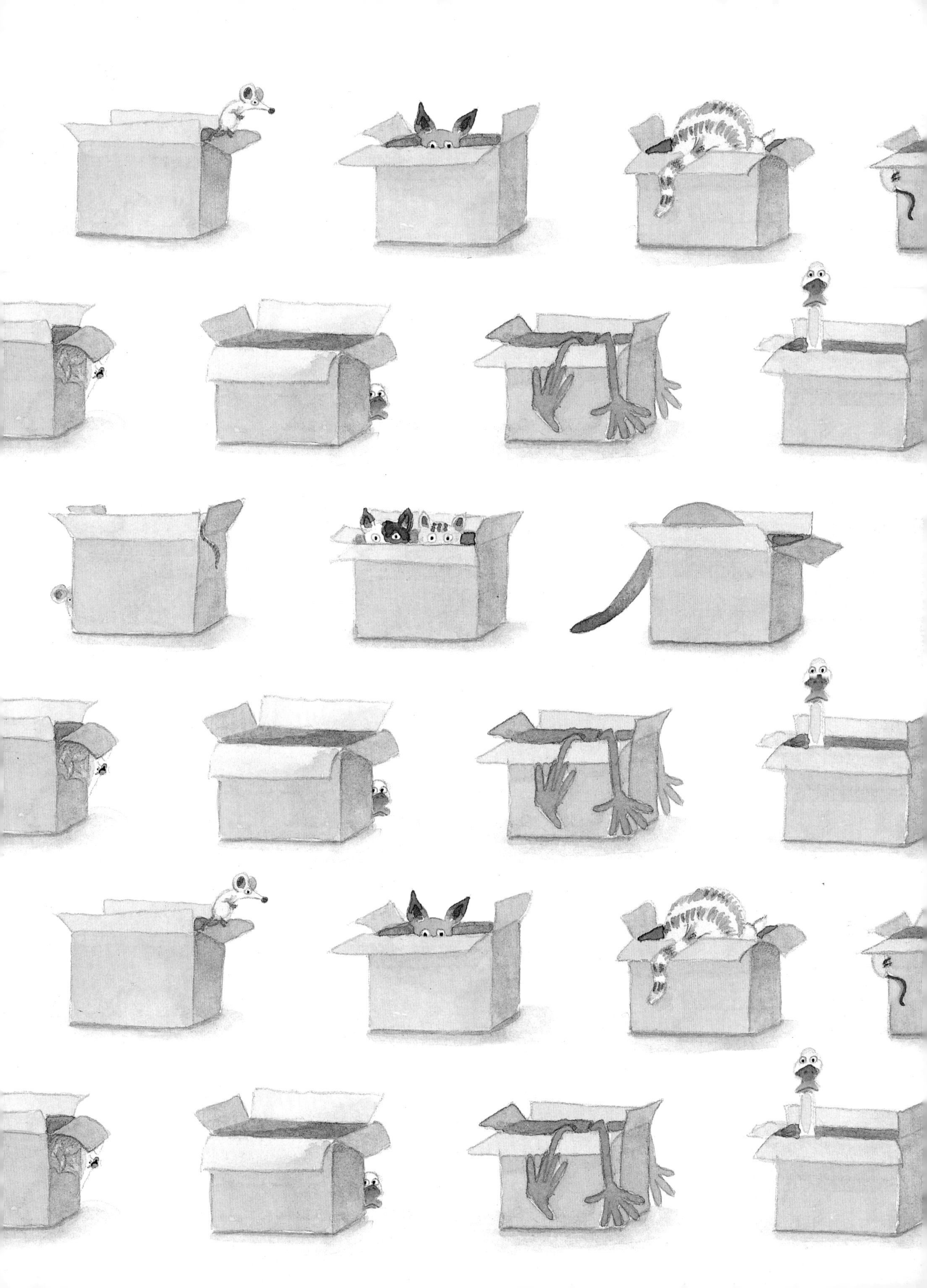